The Arabian Nights

Tales from
a Thousand and One Nights

The Arabian Nights

Tales from a Thousand and One Nights

Retold by Fiona Waters

Illustrated by Christopher Corr

Pavilion Children's Books

For Mike, who has always listened to my stories, with much love – FW

For Teresa, Sean and Liz – CC

First published in Great Britain in 2002 by
Pavilion Children's Books
A member of **Chrysalis** Books plc
64 Brewery Road
London N7 9NT
www.pavilionbooks.co.uk

Designed by Sarah Goodwin

A CIP catalogue record for this book is available
from the British Library.

ISBN 1 84365 003 7

Set in Bernhard Modern
Printed in China

2 4 6 8 10 9 7 5 3 1

This book can be ordered direct from the publisher. Please contact
the Marketing Department. But try your bookshop first.

Contents

How Sheherezade Came to Tell the Stories

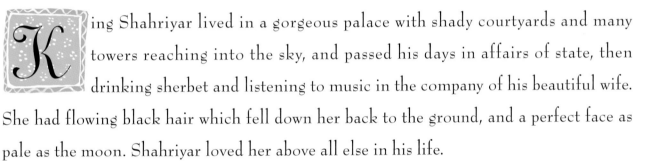

King Shahriyar lived in a gorgeous palace with shady courtyards and many towers reaching into the sky, and passed his days in affairs of state, then drinking sherbet and listening to music in the company of his beautiful wife. She had flowing black hair which fell down her back to the ground, and a perfect face as pale as the moon. Shahriyar loved her above all else in his life.

One fateful day Shahriyar decided to visit his brother Shahzaman. He bid his beautiful wife farewell and as he bent to kiss her, he pulled her veil over her face for no man other than the king himself was allowed to look on her beauty. Shahriyar was just passing through the city gates when he realized he had forgotten his present to his brother: a rare leather-bound book of magic tales (Shahriyar was very fond of tales, and you should remember that). He sped back to the palace and into his private quarters. Great was his anger when he saw his wife, with her veil flung back, talking to the Chief of the Royal Archers. And worse, the Chief of the Royal Archers was holding her hand!

In a blind rage, Shahriyar drew his dagger and plunged it deep into his wife's heart, and then he despatched the Chief of the Royal Archers in a similar fashion.

"Have the servants remove the bodies of my faithless wife and the Chief of the Royal Archers," he bellowed, and the Grand Vizier could see it was not the moment to ask what had happened.

The king was overcome with grief. He had loved his beautiful wife, with her perfect face as pale as the moon, very deeply, and could not bear to have been deceived. A great bitterness grew in his heart where before there had been only gentleness and love.

For days and days the king sat brooding, then he summoned the Grand Vizier. "I wish to marry again," he shouted.

"Most Noble King, this is wondrous news!" cried the Grand Vizier.

"Fool! There will be no rejoicing at this marriage, or the next or the next!" said Shahriyar. "I shall marry for one day only. The next morning the Royal Executioner will take my bride away and do what he does best before I am unwise enough to fall in love with her. Then I shall marry another maiden that afternoon." This was a terrible plan and the Grand Vizier did not know what to say to his king. He stood there trembling in his slippers.

"Well, what are you waiting for?" demanded Shahriyar. "Find me my first bride."

The Grand Vizier stood shaking outside the door. What could he do but obey his king's terrible order?

And so it was for two long and dreadful years. Every day the king married and the next morning the Royal Executioner took a weeping girl away. It became harder and harder to find brides.

The streets were empty of young girls and the city became a silent and sad place. In the end there was only one girl left — and that was the Grand Vizier's own daughter, Sheherezade. With an aching heart, the Grand Vizier led Sheherezade to her marriage ceremony, and then left her with Shahriyar.

"My Lord, shall I tell you a story to soothe you to sleep?" said Sheherezade, and her voice was low and musical. Shahriyar nodded and closed his eyes.

"Hear then, O King, the story of *Ali Baba and the Forty Thieves*. Once upon a far off time, there lived two brothers in an old city in Persia..." and Sheherezade spoke on through the night. But just as the sun was rising, she stopped in mid-sentence.

"Don't stop, I want to hear the rest of the story," said Shahriyar crossly.

Now Sheherezade had known very well that Shahriyar so loved stories he would find it impossible not to hear the end of her tale, but she also wished to keep her head upon her shoulders so she merely smiled graciously at the cross king.

"My Lord, it is morning. You have matters of state to attend to," said Sheherezade calmly.

"Very well then," said Shahriyar impatiently, waving the Royal Executioner away. "You may finish the tale tonight, but tomorrow I shall have you executed."

Sheherezade bowed, but said nothing. And as the stars came out that evening, she came into the king's quarters, and began speaking.

And so here is the story of *Ali Baba and the Forty Thieves*.

Ali Baba and the Forty Thieves

nce upon a far off time, there lived two brothers in an old city in Persia. Kassim, the elder brother, married a most disagreeable woman simply because she was very wealthy. Kassim grew fat and lazy, and his wife just grew more disagreeable. The younger brother, Ali Baba, was a woodcutter and he was very different to his lazy brother. He married a pretty and kind girl and they had a son called Ahmad, and an orphan girl, Morgiana, to help in the house, though in truth she was just part of the family. Ali Baba worked long hours to provide for his family but they were all well content. The fat Kassim and his disagreeable wife could have helped Ali Baba to buy a new donkey or to mend the roof when the occasion arose, but they were far too mean even to think of such a thing.

One day Ali Baba was cutting wood near a huge rock face in a part of the forest he did not know very well. It was a lonely spot and so when he heard the sound of a great troop of horses galloping towards him, Ali Baba decided very quickly that in all probability it would do him no good to be discovered

in such a place all on his own. He quietly hid his donkeys behind a thicket and then climbed deep into the leafy branches of a great tree. No sooner had he pulled his feet up out of sight than a band of wicked-looking ruffians swept up to the rock face. They were all armed to the teeth with daggers and great curved scimitars, and they wore rough black cloaks. Ali Baba counted thirty-nine of them, and then a man who was obviously the captain galloped up on a big snorting black horse. All the horses were heavily laden, and once the men had dismounted they piled their bulging saddlebags up against the foot of the rock.

Then the captain strode up to the rock face. In a great and terrible voice he called out, *"Open sesame!"* and before Ali Baba's astonished eyes a huge door, cut deep into the rock, opened up. The men all marched in and, when every single one was inside, the captain followed and called out again, *"Shut sesame!"* and it was as if they had never been there. The rock face was as smooth as before.

Ali Baba's knees were trembling. He realized the fierce captain would show him no mercy were he discovered. He decided to remain hidden, praying all the while that his donkeys would keep silent. To his great relief it was not long before the door opened again and the men all came streaming out, clutching their now empty saddlebags. They mounted up again and the entire band galloped away as noisily as they had arrived. The dust settled and silence reigned again in the forest.

After waiting until he was quite sure that they were all long gone, Ali Baba scrambled down the tree and ran to check on his donkeys. But then his curiosity overcame his fear. Whatever could be hidden in the cave? He stepped gingerly up to the rock. It was as smooth as marble and nowhere could Ali Baba see even the finest crack that might be a door.

"There is magic here, undoubtedly," he thought to himself, "but all the captain said was the name of a grain that my wife uses to make cakes," and so the trembling Ali Baba whispered, "*Open sesame*, please?" To his utter astonishment, the door opened with a quiet rumble. "It can't do any harm to have a quick look," he said to himself, and he stepped into the cave.

It took a moment for his eyes to get used to the dim light which filtered in through slits in the roof but then he saw the most breathtaking sight. Far from being an empty and dreary cavern, Ali Baba saw that he had walked into a treasure house. Huge chests overflowed with gold and silver tureens and plates, and finely worked jugs and goblets. Precious stones, rubies, emeralds and sapphires stained the rough rock with rainbow lights and strings of pearls gleamed like small moons. Sacks of coins spilled onto the floor,

and necklaces of diamonds and finely decorated crowns were all tumbled together anyhow. Bales of precious silks and brocades were strewn everywhere and rare carpets and rugs were rolled up carelessly along the walls. The cave had obviously been the storehouse for many generations of thieves.

Ali Baba was speechless, but then his wits began to reassemble themselves. "Allah be praised, now I shall be able to provide for my family for years to come! But I must make haste lest the thieves return," he murmured. What to take? That was the question. Ali Baba decided that a few bags of gold coins might be the safest thing. No one would notice if he very carefully spent a gold coin now and again. So he took two small bags of coins from an open sack right at the back of the cave where he thought the loss might not be detected, and closing the rock door behind him, said, *"Shut sesame!"* and went back home.

Ali Baba could not contain his excitement as he told his wife all about the cave and the thieves and the bags of gold. Well, she was overjoyed but when she saw the gold coins tumbling from the bags she grew frightened.

"This is too much to leave lying around, Ali Baba! We must keep out a little and bury the rest under the house. I shall go and borrow a measure from our sister-in-law so we know how much we have hidden," she said.

"You are the wisest of wives," smiled Ali Baba, "but make sure you don't let her know what it is we want to measure!"

Now you will remember that Kassim's wife was a most disagreeable woman. Not only was she disagreeable, but she was sneaky and mean as well. Being sneaky, she could not help but wonder what it was that Ali Baba had in such quantity that he needed to measure it. So she rubbed a little wax under the base of the measure before giving it to her sister-in-law.

When she reached home, the first thing Ali Baba's wife did was to put the measure on top of the great shining pile of gold coins, and thus it was their secret was revealed! Ali Baba and his wife measured all the gold, and, after burying it carefully, took the measure back to Kassim's wife. You can imagine her rage when she found a gold coin stuck to the bottom. She ran to Kassim and told him that surely Allah had frowned on them, for why should Ali Baba and his family have such wealth bestowed on them? Instead of being happy for his brother, Kassim grew cold with envy and spite and he wasted no time in rushing round to Ali Baba. "Deceitful and worthless object! How dare you keep such a secret from me!" he shouted. "Tell me at once how you come to have so much gold that you need a measure to count it!" And Kassim threatened to tell everyone that his own brother was a thief if Ali Baba did not share his new-found wealth.

So Ali Baba told the whole story. "But if we are cautious, the thieves will never know their secret has been discovered, and we can live comfortably for the rest of our days."

However, Kassim was determined to have the lion's share of the treasure. The next morning he set off for the cave with twenty donkeys, each carrying two empty baskets. When he stood in front of the rock face he roared, *"Open sesame!"* and the great door opened.

Kassim could not believe his greedy eyes when he saw the sacks of coins, the bracelets, the goblets, the strings of pearls, the silks and brocades. He shouted at the door again, *"Shut sesame!"* so he might not be disturbed and began to collect great heaps of treasure to take away. All the while he was muttering to himself. "Twenty donkeys? Ha! I need a hundred donkeys. I shall soon have this place cleared out," and there was a great deal more of such foolish talk as Kassim huffed and puffed his way around the cave, for you will remember he was very fat. No sooner had he pulled out a fabulous silver crown than he saw a remarkable golden platter and threw the crown to one side. But eventually he had filled his forty baskets, and then a terrible fear gripped him for he found he had forgotten the magic words to open the door once again.

"Open barley!" he cried.

But the door did not budge.

"Open wheat!"

"Open millet!"

But the door remained firmly shut.

Then Kassim began to tremble from head to foot for outside he could hear the thundering of many horses' hooves. The thieves had come back!

"Open sesame!" roared a terrible voice, and as the door opened there stood the captain, his scimitar gleaming in his hand and the fearsome band of ruffians at his back. Kassim squeaked with terror and fell to his knees. The thieves laughed at this miserable burglar and very quickly chopped him into six pieces. And that was the end of Kassim.

Then they emptied the unfortunate Kassim's baskets and looked round the cave to see if anything else was missing. Of course they did not notice the few gold coins that Ali Baba had taken and so they were satisfied that Kassim alone knew the secret of their cave. They departed as swiftly as they had arrived, but they left Kassim's body behind as a warning to anyone else foolish enough to try to steal the treasure.

Meanwhile Kassim's wife was waiting at home, planning when she might wear the fabulous necklaces and rings that Kassim had promised her. But as it grew dark, she began to think that perhaps something had gone wrong, so she went round to Ali Baba's house and demanded that he go to look for his brother. Ali Baba took one of his donkeys and went off to the forest in search of Kassim. It did not take him long to discover the terrible truth, and unkind and heartless though Kassim had always been, Ali Baba wept for his brother.

"The very least I can now do is to give you a decent burial, brother," sobbed Ali Baba as he wrapped Kassim as well as he could in an old cloak he found at the back of the cave. Of course Ali Baba realized very well that by taking Kassim's body away he was letting the thieves know that someone else did indeed know their secret but he could not just leave him there. And so Ali Baba went sadly home.

The next problem was how to arrange the funeral without any awkward questions being asked. It was not the custom of the city to be buried in a coffin, but to be wrapped in special silken cloths – rather tricky for a body chopped into six pieces. The resourceful Morgiana came up with the solution. In the bazaar there was a poor old cobbler, Baba Mustafa, who was known for his fine needlework. Morgiana went to the bazaar with all speed and when she had sought out Baba Mustafa she took him to one side and slipped one of the gold coins from the cave into his hand. "There is plenty more where that came from, O most excellent of cobblers. My master has great need of your services, but it is a matter of the utmost secrecy and delicacy."

The cobbler put aside the slippers he was sewing, and even agreed to Morgiana's demand that she blindfold him as they hurried back to Ali Baba's house. When he saw what was required of him, Baba Mustafa raised his eyebrows right up into his turban, but another gold coin soon persuaded him to take out his needle and thread and start sewing. When he had finished his unusual task, Morgiana blindfolded Baba Mustafa once more and led him back to the bazaar. Thus restored to one piece, Kassim was buried with all due respect and Ali Baba went back to work, although he was careful not to go anywhere near the cave in the forest.

But, of course, the thieves soon discovered that their secret had not died with Kassim. When they came back to find his body gone, they were furious but also puzzled. Who would take away a dead body yet leave all the treasure behind? The captain decided to venture into the bazaar, disguised as a merchant, to see if anyone knew anything about a body that had been cut into six pieces. By extreme ill fortune, the first person the captain spoke to was none other than Baba Mustafa who was sitting cross-legged in his shop, sewing a pair of golden slippers.

"You must have remarkably good eyes to sew such tiny stitches," said the supposed merchant.

"Yes indeed, Allah is good to me," smiled Baba Mustafa. "He has given me exceptionally keen eyesight. But I can do better than these little slippers. Why, recently I was asked to sew together six pieces of a dead body!"

"How very curious," murmured the supposed merchant, and his eyes glittered with triumph. "And where was it you performed this remarkable feat?" he asked.

"I was blindfolded so I don't really know," answered Baba Mustafa, "but there was a very strong smell of spices so I imagine it must have been near the spice stalls."

"I am sure you would be able to find your way there again. I would so like to see the house where such an interesting thing took place," said the merchant.

And so by a mixture of flattery and bribery (for the captain had taken the precaution of showing Baba Mustafa the heavy bag of gold that hung from his belt) the two of them stepped out into the narrow lanes that surrounded the bazaar. Sometimes the Fates are not kind, and this day they were not smiling on Ali Baba, for after many false turns and dead ends Baba Mustafa led the captain to Ali Baba's house!

"This must be it," cried Baba Mustafa in triumph, "I remember that broken third step down into the house." The captain gave Baba Mustafa several gold pieces, who by now was thinking that perhaps he should set up in business as a stitcher-up-of-bodies, so profitable was it proving to be. As they parted company, the captain noted very carefully where the house was situated.

The next evening as Ali Baba came home, he saw a man with a great long white beard and flowing white robes leading a string of donkeys up the street. Each of the donkeys was carrying two wide oil flagons on either side of its saddle. When the procession drew close to Ali Baba's house, the man bowed courteously and spoke. "Honoured Master, I am a travelling oil merchant seeking shelter for the night. In your very great kindness if you were able to accommodate me, Allah would indeed shower blessings upon your head."

Ali Baba, of course, welcomed the man into his house and they were soon sitting enjoying an excellent supper. The oil merchant seemed to have had a most interesting life and had travelled in many fabled lands. But Morgiana was suspicious of the smooth-talking stranger, and so when he went out to see to his donkeys in the yard, she followed and hid in the shadows. He went up to each donkey in turn and whispered, "When I strike the lid be ready!" Then he returned indoors and regaled Ali Baba with more of his stories.

Morgiana went back to prepare the coffee, puzzling all the while what the stranger was up to. She was just about to serve the coffee when the lamp in the kitchen went out. She had forgotten to buy any more oil but then she remembered the oil flagons on the donkeys. She ran out with her ladle and, opening the first jar, went to take out some oil. She nearly dropped the ladle in fright when a deep voice muttered, "Is it time, Captain?" and a figure began to unwind itself from inside. She understood immediately. Hidden inside each flagon must be one of the thirty-nine thieves! She kept her wits about her. "Not yet!" she growled in as deep a voice as she could manage, and pushed the thief back down into the flagon. She checked every one of the flagons and only the last one really did contain oil. Then she slipped away.

Morgiana served the coffee to Ali Baba and the smooth-talking traveller who, of course, was none other than the captain of the thieves. She went back to the kitchen and put her biggest cooking pot onto the fire. She brought in the real flagon of oil from outside and poured it all into her cooking pot. As soon as the oil was bubbling, she took the cooking pot out into the yard. She very carefully opened up each flagon and swiftly poured some oil over every single one of the robbers, and that was the end of them!

But Morgiana had not finished yet. She tiptoed up into her room and swiftly took off her everyday clothes. She draped herself with all manner of scarves, and put her best slippers of crimson leather on her feet. Last of all, she slipped a small dagger under one of the scarves. You can imagine Ali Baba's surprise when a few moments later she twirled into the room where he and the oil merchant were still sitting over their coffee. Morgiana began a slow dance round the room. Ali Baba thought she had taken leave of her senses. Round and round she circled, scarves floating behind her, getting ever nearer to the delighted oil merchant. Suddenly she swooped, and plunged the dagger deep into his heart!

Ali Baba leapt to his feet, absolutely horrified. "Morgiana, what have you done?" he shrieked. Ali Baba's wife and Ahmad came running. What a sight met their eyes! Morgiana with a bloodstained dagger in her hand, Ali Baba tearing his hair out and a very large dead man lying on the floor. But Morgiana bent down and pulled off the long white beard and there was the captain of the thieves.

"Wisest of women, O, many are the thanks I must shower on your head," cried Ali Baba. "We are indeed blessed to have you under our roof. Without your perspicacity and wisdom we should all be lying dead in our beds," and on and on he went in a similar vein. (You must remember he had just had a very great fright.)

The next morning before it was really light, Ali Baba lead the donkeys, still carrying the oil flagons and the very large bundle that was the captain, to the top of a steep precipice that dropped down to a swiftly flowing river. There he rolled the oil flagons and the very large bundle over the edge and that was the end of the forty thieves. Many, many moons later he went to the cave where he found grass all grown over the entrance, so he knew no one else had been there in a very long while. Over the years he took a little gold at a time, just enough for their needs, and he and his family and the indomitable Morgiana lived for many years in great contentment and not a little comfort. But they were always ready to shelter weary travellers, providing Morgiana approved of them, of course!

The Man Who Stole the Dish of Gold

ow in the old city of Baghdad there lived a wealthy merchant called Ja'afar. He lived in a fine house with shady marble courtyards piled high with gorgeous silk cushions, where fountains splashed cooling perfumed water. Ja'afar had many beautiful wives and a host of happy children and he was well content. But how quickly the Lord of Fates may turn his hand! There came a terrible day when Ja'afar learnt that all his camel trains had been lost in the desert, his traders had fled and his coffers were utterly empty. Ja'afar decided he must go out and seek work himself. So he put on an ancient robe that belonged to his second gardener and left with the avowed intention of not returning until he had restored his fortunes.

He wandered for many months until he reached a city of tall walls and mighty gates. He was frail from lack of food, he was filthy dirty and the second gardener's robe was tattered and torn.

27

As he wandered the streets aimlessly, Ja'afar became aware that everyone else was hurrying in one direction. His curiosity was aroused and so he turned around and joined the crowd. Before long he found himself in front of a great palace. He felt so poor and shabby that his courage failed him at the gate and he turned aside, but the throng entering was so great that he was swept along, through the golden gate and into a vast room hung with rich rugs of glowing colours and lit by many glittering candles. Ja'afar gazed around, utterly spellbound. Great golden suns and silver moons were floating above his head, suspended from the midnight blue ceiling and the floor was of black marble which reflected the sparkle of the candles. Dark-eyed girls played on silver flutes and servants offered dishes of sugared almonds to all the guests.

Presently Ja'afar saw a splendidly attired courtier leading in four sleek hunting dogs with gleaming coats and golden collars about their necks. Each dog had his own tasselled rug and set on each rug was a golden dish, filled with chunks of delicious-smelling meat. Poor Ja'afar licked his cracked lips as his empty stomach rumbled. One of the dogs looked directly at Ja'afar and raised a delicate paw to push the golden dish towards him, its huge brown eyes never leaving his. It seemed to be offering Ja'afar the food to eat. Ja'afar looked over his shoulder but everyone else was far too busy to notice so he accepted the dog's generous offer and began to eat. He was careful to leave some for the dog, but again the noble creature pushed the dish towards Ja'afar, so he soon licked the dish clean. He bowed to the dog and went to turn away, but for a third time the dog pushed the dish towards Ja'afar and he realized the dog wished him to take the golden dish as well. He wrapped it in his tattered rags and left the palace and the city with the tall walls and mighty gates. Allah had provided for him and his days of shame were over.

He soon reached another city where he sold the golden dish for a great many gold pieces and bought fine leather hides and two rare rugs which he sold to a passing sultan. And with the profits he was able to buy more rugs and several camels, and so he journeyed home at last to his beautiful wives and his host of children. You can imagine the rejoicing! And day by day his fortune grew and soon Ja'afar was even richer than he had ever been before.

But he never forgot the hunting dog, and he determined to return to the city with the tall walls and mighty gates and seek out the palace so he might repay the generosity that had been shown to him. He went to the bazaar and purchased a great golden dish which he filled with rare spices and then he wrapped the dish in a finely woven rug from Tashkent. And so he journeyed back to the city of tall walls and mighty gates, and this time he strode boldly down the wide street towards the palace. His heart was full of

delight at the thought of how he might settle his debt, but he
came to a sudden halt. Where the palace had been there was
nothing but a smoking, crumbling ruin. Vultures flew in and out
of the empty walls and desolation hung over everything. Kneeling
in the ashes was a weeping man, and Ja'afar asked him what had
happened to the palace and the golden suns and silver moons,
the dark-eyed girls playing the silver flutes and the sleek hunting
dogs. The man told Ja'afar he had owned the palace but a great fire had
destroyed everything. How quickly the Lord of Fates had turned his hand!

Ja'afar rolled out the rug from Tashkent and bid the man, whose name was Hasan, sit
while he told his tale. Hasan, of course, did not believe Ja'afar at first, no one could be so
honest, but eventually he was convinced. And, although Hasan became as a brother to
Ja'afar, he would not accept the golden dish as he knew it was Allah's will that he be humbled
for his ostentation in having his dogs eat off golden dishes. And to this day the golden dish
is locked in a cabinet in Ja'afar's house as a reminder of the need for humility.

The Half-Lie

he sun was beating down on the bustling bazaar. Abou Hassan, the merchant, mopped his brow. He was hot and tired, and he badly needed a cup of strong black coffee, but he still had to find one more servant for his wife, the formidable Nuzet. She had decided that she needed someone to walk her pet pea-hen. Abou Hassan thought this was nonsense, but one look at his scowling wife convinced him that a peaceable life was only to be maintained if she had her servant to walk her pet pea-hen. He had already purchased a new cook and a third gardener for her that day, but he knew he could not rest until a pea-hen walker was in the servants' quarters.

There was one dealer left in the corner. He had a single man slouched at the end of a rather frayed rope.

"How much for this feeble excuse of a personage?" asked Abou Hassan looking down his nose.

"Only six hundred pieces of silver," said the dealer ingratiatingly, "for he has one fault."

Now this was indeed very cheap, but Abou Hassan was not one to do a deal without a bit of haggling.

"And what might this fault be, impudent dealer in second-rate merchandise?"

"He tells one lie a year, and there is no way of stopping him," replied the dealer.

"One lie a year?" smirked Abou Hassan. "One lie a year? Why, you do yourself down, you son of a misbegotten ratbag. I would think all of my servants tell me one lie a *day*. I will take him," and Abou Hassan slapped the money down before the dealer could retract his offer.

Abou Hassan had his cup of strong black coffee while the feeble excuse of a personage, who was actually called Akil,
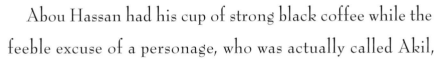
stood patiently in the dusty street. And then they went home. Nuzet was delighted with her new cook and the third gardener, but she was not so sure of Akil.

"Why should he be so cheap?" she demanded, for Abou Hassan had not mentioned the one lie a year bit.

"O, wife, are you so blind to the endless talents of your remarkable husband? He is so cheap because I drove a very hard bargain with the rascally dealer," said Abou Hassan, with his fingers crossed behind his back. For a while all seemed well. Akil did actually work very hard, not only at walking the pea-hen, which in truth was not so demanding, but he found other jobs to do about the house and he was soon the delight of even the sour Nuzet.

It was the time of the New Year celebrations and Abou Hassan and his friends had gone out of the dusty city to an oasis where the flowers bloomed in great profusion and the sound of running water was restful on the ears. Akil carried a picnic of wine and fruit and the small sweet cakes that Abou Hassan was so fond of. They had not been long settled on soft cushions and carpets, sipping the wine and nibbling the cakes, when Abou Hassan ordered Akil to go back home and fetch the pistachio nuts that had been forgotten in the confusion of leaving. Akil set off with a smile, but as he passed through the city gates and drew closer to Abou Hassan's house, he began to wail and cry, beating his forehead with his fists.

"O, my dear Master, alas, alas! What will become of us all now without him?" and he tore his clothes and threw dirt on his body. "What will become of us now?"

Soon there was quite a crowd following the distressed Akil and as he turned into Abou Hassan's street, the noise reached the ears of Nuzet, who flung open the door with a cross look on her face.

"Akil!" she shouted above the din, "What is the meaning of this?"

"O, my most noble Mistress! Woe is your humble servant that I should be the bearer of such terrible news. Woe! Woe!" cried Akil.

"What is the terrible news?" thundered Nuzet.

"Most revered Mistress, may my tongue be shrivelled as I tell you that your husband, the gracious Abou Hassan, is dead," sobbed Akil.

"Dead?" shrieked Nuzet. "O, indeed twice woe, what will become of us all now?" and she began to tear her clothes as she stumbled back inside the house.

In her great grief, she ran through the house, smashing the china as she went, for that was how you showed respect for the dead in Abou Hassan's day.

"Come, Akil, help me tear down the tapestries and pour away the wine. I must show respect for my much-lamented husband," she wailed.

Akil set to with great energy and before long the house was completely ruined. Broken china and glass littered the floor, feathers from the great divan cushions blew everywhere and the furniture was smashed to smithereens. Abou Hassan's favourite coffee cups were ground to dust, and even the pet pea-hen was swept out of the door in a flurry of squawking.

"Now, dear Akil, you must lead me to my husband's body that I may bring him back for burial," Nuzet said, her voice muffled by the great veil behind which she had hidden her face.

So a sad procession set off through the streets, and out of the city gates. All the other wives had joined Nuzet, together with the cook and the first, second *and* third gardeners, with Akil at the head of the wailing group. Akil kept up a steady stream of howling and weeping and tearing of his clothes, but he walked faster than the others and he was soon quite some distance from Nuzet and her fellow mourners.

For a while, Akil walked in silence. Then he began wailing and shouting again, but this time he was crying, "O, my dear Mistress! O, woe, woe. What will become of me without her?" and he beat his chest as he ran towards the oasis.

Before too long an angry Abou Hassan bustled up to the wailing servant. "Pull yourself together, O, snivelling worm. Whatever is the matter?"

"O, may Allah be merciful to us all, my Master! When I reached your house to collect the pistachio nuts, I found the entire house had collapsed and everyone was crushed inside!" wept Akil.

"All crushed?" asked the stunned Abou Hassan. "My wife and my children, too?"

"All," whispered Akil.

Abou Hassan turned pale.

"My donkey, and my hens and the goats?"

"All," whispered Akil.

Then Abou Hassan began to yell his grief, too, and he tore off his turban and stamped it on the dusty ground. His friends joined him and all began beating their chests and weeping. Slowly they started off back towards the city. Of course, it was not too long before they saw another crowd of mourners heading in their direction. As they grew closer, they began to recognize each other.

"Is that you, my precious petal?" asked Abou Hassan, looking at the veiled figure who did very much resemble his wife.

"Can that be you, my husband and provider?" asked Nuzet, looking at the turban-less figure approaching through the dust.

They embraced and then both turned slowly to look at Akil who was standing there, astonishingly, with a huge grin on his face.

"What's this, what's this, you wretched son of a one-eyed thief?" shouted Abou Hassan. "You cause all this distress and mayhem, and then you have the double impertinence to grin at us?"

"You shall be flogged from Here to There and Back Again," hissed Nuzet, who was feeling decidedly ill at the thought of the mess back home.

"Ah!" said Akil, grinning even more. "But that would not be fair, my Mistress. Perhaps you did not know," he said – knowing full well that she most certainly did not – "perhaps you did not know that your husband bought me cheap because I had one fault."

Abou Hassan turned as red as he had previously turned pale. Nuzet was clearly working herself up to a huge rage.

"Yes, well, perhaps I shall have to overlook the lie this year," spluttered Abou Hassan.

"That seems only fair, Master," smiled Akil, "but I have to tell you that this was only half a lie. Before the next New Year I shall tell you the other half!"

Abou Hassan was livid, and Nuzet was beside herself, but all the others said it would not be fair to punish Akil, as a deal was a deal. So they walked slowly back to the city gates. But when Abou Hassan reached his house and saw the damage Akil had caused, he shrieked, "Half a lie? You call this half a lie?

Whatever would you do for a whole lie? Lay waste to an entire village? I do not wish to find out, I can promise you here and now! Get out of my sight, you are released from our deal," and he pushed the still-grinning Akil out of what was left of the front door and collapsed onto a shredded cushion. Nuzet plumped down beside him and they gazed at the destruction all around them.

"Well, wife..." began Abou Hassan.

"Well, husband..." began Nuzet.

And they both burst out laughing. Never again did Nuzet demand someone to walk her pet pea-hen, and never again did Abou Hassan buy a cheap servant. And it is said they lived in great contentment ever after!

Prince Agib

 he Prince Agib, son of King Khasib, had embarked on a long voyage There and Back Again to see how far it was. He was a great adventurer and was always in search of new delights. He and his sailors had been at sea for many long weeks, sailing far into the unknown, when one day all of a sudden a thick fog descended upon the ship like a curtain. The sails hung limply and not a sound was to be heard. The captain looked round fearfully.

"Noble Prince, I have a very great fear that this is no ordinary fog but one conjured up by a djinn. We must give ourselves up for lost."

"O, feeble-minded slave, where is your courage?" retorted Prince Agib crossly. "Who knows what we shall see when this fog clears!" and he ran to the telescope to see if anything at all was visible through the fog. But all he saw was an impenetrable, murky wall. Days passed, and the captain was reduced to a quivering jelly, but Prince Agib raised the telescope again, seeking some break in the fog. And then it happened. As swiftly as it had fallen, the fog disappeared, and there in front of the ship rose a huge mountain of black stone. The current was swift and the boat hurtled

towards the foot of the mountain and seeming sure destruction. But just as everyone, including the bold Prince Agib, had their eyes tightly shut in expectation of a mighty crunch, something entirely different happened. Every single nail and everything else that was made of iron flew towards the mountain. The ship collapsed in a heap of timber, and everyone was flung into the water. Prince Agib made it to the shore, but it seemed the captain had been right, everyone else was lost. Prince Agib managed to pull himself out of the crashing surf and onto a rocky ledge where he lay gasping for breath.

As he lay there he heard a strange voice whisper in his ear, "O, Great Son of Khasib, hear and obey. The black stone mountain you see is a loadstone, which is why your ship fell to pieces, for all iron is pulled towards the stone. You must climb the mountain and at the very top you will find an immense statue of a horseman, forged entirely out of brass. Destroy the statue and the sea will rise up to cover the whole island forever and you will have rid the seas of this scourge."

Well, Prince Agib was very willing to try. "But how on earth am I to destroy an immense statue of brass?" he thought to himself as he squeezed the water out of his boots.

"Provision has been made, O Great Son of Khasib. At the foot of the mountain you will find a bow of brass and three arrows of lead. With these weapons you will destroy the horseman," whispered the strange voice again.

42

So Prince Agib scrambled to his feet and made his way

to the foot of the mountain where, sure enough, he found the bow of brass

and the three arrows of lead. It took him a long time to climb the black mountain but

just as the sun was setting he reached the summit. The statue was absolutely huge and

Prince Agib did not see how his feeble weapons were going to destroy it, but he strung the

brass bow and let the first lead arrow fly. It flew true but bounced harmlessly off the

horseman. Prince Agib took up the second arrow, but the same thing happened again.

With a sinking heart he placed the last arrow in the bow. How could he possibly destroy

the horseman with just his bare hands? He held the arrow taut, then let it go with a great

twang. Straight it flew, and hit the statue of the horseman square in the chest. There was

a mighty rumbling sound and before his astonished eyes, the statue crumbled away,

leaving only a fine pile of dust at Prince Agib's feet. He whirled round to look at the sea.

A gigantic wave, taller than the mast of the finest vessel in his father's shipyard, was

rolling towards the shore. In seconds, the wave covered the island, the black mountain

and Prince Agib completely. He struggled for a moment, water roaring in his ears, but

then he fell into a swoon and knew no more.

Far away from the island of the black stone mountain, there was another island. This was a beautiful island, covered in green forests and lush meadows full of elegant horses. Hummingbirds flew in and out of huge perfumed lilies, haughty peacocks fanned their tails as they wafted along the paths and butterflies flitted from orchid to orchid. In the middle of the island was a gorgeous palace of white marble. The sun glittered off its many minarets and the fountains splashed with sparkling blue water. Smartly attired servants bustled about, and over the sound of the fountains could be heard the sound of much giggling. The palace had belonged to a mighty sultan but when he reached a great age he had died and left all his wealth to his daughters, and there were many of them! They now lived in splendid style with not a care in the world. A few days before, the island had been washed by a bigger than usual tide, but no one paid very much attention.

The youngest daughter, who was called Purest Pearl, was wandering along the shore, dipping her toes into the water as she spotted a particularly lovely shell. (She collected shells and had whole rooms given over to their display.) She had a very small servant with her to carry all the shells, and he was staggering with the weight of Purest Pearl's latest collection. She stopped suddenly with a shriek. There was the body of a young man lying on the sand. It was Prince Agib.

The very small servant was sent back to the palace with all speed, still carrying the shells as Purest Pearl was not going to leave them behind. Soon Prince Agib was hoisted onto a litter and taken back to the palace where all the daughters crowded round him as he lay on a couch.

"Ooo! Poor thing! Is he dead?" cooed one.

"Take off his boots, his dear feet must be soaking!" ordered another.

"I shall sing him a song of recovery," trilled the eldest daughter.

"He is so handsome, I am sure he must be a king's son," and so on and so on. Not surprisingly with all this noise going on, Prince Agib – who was not at all dead, merely somewhat wet and very battered and bruised – was soon awake again. He sat up.

"Ooooo!" squealed all the daughters at once.

"Please don't do that," said Prince Agib, putting his hands over his ears. "I am very grateful to be rescued, but could you please not squeal quite so loudly?" and he smiled at the startled daughters. Of course, they were all enchanted by him and nothing was too much trouble. He was fed apricots and dates stuffed with marzipan. A goblet of deep red wine was always by his side, and new clothes of the costliest silk appeared every morning in his dressing-room. His bath was scented with rare perfumes and rose petals floated on the surface, and he even had a servant just to iron his handkerchiefs. The daughters sang to him and danced for him, and he wanted for nothing.

One day the eldest daughter came to him and said, "Dear Prince Agib, we have to go away for forty days and we cannot take you with us. You are most welcome to stay here until we return. Here are the keys to the palace, one hundred in number, and you can explore as you will. But on no account must you open the hundredth door, the door of red gold. If you do, it will be the worse for you, and for us all," and so the daughters and a great retinue of servants departed.

The next morning Prince Agib began to explore the palace. He opened a great many doors and found a room full of rubies and emeralds and a room full of singing canaries and a room full of jasmine and narcissus, and he did not give the door of red gold – the hundredth door – a thought. The following day he opened many more doors and found a room full of jars of wild honey and a room full of musical instruments, all being played by unseen hands. He found a room full of maps where the rivers flowed with real water and the winds blew off the chart, and a room full of dancing cats and a room full of swaying towers of candied chestnuts, and as he ate his supper he thought, "Whatever can be behind the door of red gold, the hundredth door? I have seen more wonders than I ever thought to see." When he went to bed he was unsettled.

On the third morning when he woke up, the first thing he thought of was the door of red gold, the hundredth door. "It can't do any harm just to look at it," he thought, and so he went and stood in front of the door. It looked just like the other ninety-nine doors except it was red gold. He wandered off and opened a few more doors. He found a room full of chickens laying golden eggs and a room full of books that were all talking to each other and a room full of flying fish but he was no longer interested in such ordinary things. "What could be the harm in just having a look behind the door of red gold?" he wondered, and then found his feet had taken him to the very door. He looked over his shoulder. There was no one about, so he took the great bunch of keys and turned the lock in the door of red gold, the hundredth door. He looked over his shoulder again, still no one, and so very slowly he opened the door, the fateful hundredth door. There was a blinding flash of light, a huge clap of thunder and with a great swoosh of smoke a huge djinn rushed out of the room with a wild laugh. Everything went dark and the air was filled with a terrible smell.

Alas for Prince Agib, when the smoke cleared he was sitting in the middle of a vast empty desert. The gorgeous palace of white marble with the sun glittering off its many minarets and the fountains splashing with sparkling blue water had disappeared utterly. And although he wandered through many lands for the rest of his life, Prince Agib never found it again. Sometimes he thought he heard the far-off sound of giggling but he was always disappointed.

The History of Codadad and his Brothers

The Sultan of Harran was much beloved by his subjects. His country was peaceful and efficiently run, his people all well fed and content. He had not fought a battle for many years and the coffers in the palace were overflowing with golden dinars. But the sultan had no interest in the dinars, all he wanted was a son and heir. He prayed and prayed every night, but his prayers went unanswered for many years.

Then one night a wise old prophet appeared to him in a dream. "Good Sultan, Allah is well pleased with your devotion to your people and your country, you may have what you so desire. When you rise in the morning go into the gardens of the palace and walk down the Avenue of Tranquillity. At the end of the avenue you will find an old pomegranate tree. Pick the largest fruit you can see and eat as many of the seeds as you wish. Then you will gain your reward."

In the morning the sultan rushed downstairs and out into the garden as soon as he awoke. He picked the biggest pomegranate and counted out fifty seeds into his hand. He swallowed them all, and returned to the palace with a spring in his step. That day he ordered a public holiday for everyone. It was not long before the news broke that forty-nine of his wives had each given birth to a fine young son. Great was the rejoicing in the palace, and the sultan went about with a huge smile on his face – which shows how very pleased he really was, as the sound of forty-nine babies all wailing at the same time was a little hard to bear. The soothsayer went about with silken tassels stuffed in his ears, and feathers were laid in all the

corridors so that no footfall might wake the boys when they finally fell asleep.

Only one room in the palace was utterly quiet. Pirouze, the sultan's fiftieth wife, remained childless. Great was her sadness, and, of course, she became very unhappy being surrounded by so many healthy and noisy babies. The sultan could not bear to see her suffering and suggested she go to stay with her brother in far-off Samaria. But he should have remembered that his sons were a gift from Allah who is always even-handed in his giving. Pirouze had not been with her brother for more than a few moons when she gave birth to a handsome and healthy boy. She called him Codadad but, as she felt rather estranged from the court, she did not let the sultan know about the baby's arrival.

54

Many years passed and Codadad grew into a most agreeable young man. He had all his mother's grace and virtue, and all his father's wisdom and generosity of spirit. Codadad was an accomplished horseman and could shoot an arrow straight as a die. But he was bored. He wanted to serve his father and prove his entitlement to a place at court like his forty-nine brothers. Pirouze was not at all keen, for she feared for his safety, but finally Codadad persuaded her to let him ride to the sultan to offer his services. It was decided that he should go in disguise so he could truly be judged on his merits. He dyed his hair and stained his face so he looked much older than his years.

He certainly cut an awesome figure as his great white horse galloped through the mighty gates of Harran. He wore a cloak of pure white silk, lined in the palest shimmering green, and buckled round his waist he carried a glinting scimitar of gold. His bow lay across the saddle and a quiver of silver-tipped arrows was slung across his back. The sultan welcomed him warmly as he was clearly a person of some standing, and Codadad soon became a trusted and valued courtier. His forty-nine brothers were not impressed. In a hundred simple ways, without meaning to, Codadad showed them up to be lazy and mean-spirited. The sultan praised Codadad even more and made him governor over his brothers to try to make them more disciplined and hard-working. And still no one, not even the sultan, realized who Codadad really was. It was not long before the brothers were plotting how best to get rid of Codadad.

"We need to be careful how we do this, my brothers," said one. "This Codadad is much admired by our father. We must not be seen to harm him in any way."

"Yes, but we must act soon," muttered another. "I am exhausted."

"Soon we will have no power left ourselves at all," shouted another.

And so the arguments went on. Finally it was decided that the brothers would seek Codadad's blessing to go out for a day's hunting and, once far enough away from the palace, they would find somewhere to hide so the sultan might think them lost. Then Codadad would surely get the blame for their disappearance.

The brothers all went to Codadad and begged to be allowed to go hunting for a day, promising to return in the evening. Codadad saw no harm in their request and so the very next day, with a great deal of unnecessary noise and fuss, the brothers set off on their supposed hunting trip.

As night fell there was no sign of them and before long the sultan was asking where his sons were. Codadad told the sultan where they had gone, and added, "I am sure they have merely gone further than they intended, O Noble Sultan, and will return as soon as it is light."

But, of course, there was no sign of the brothers the next morning, or the next. The sultan was furious and, in his defence, deeply upset that his precious sons were missing. As the wicked brothers had planned, he blamed Codadad and on the morning of the fourth day he summoned Codadad to his presence. "Ungrateful man!" he thundered. "I took you into my home and my family, gave you authority to look after my sons, and what is my reward? My precious sons all missing at one fell swoop. You must find them immediately or your own life will be forfeited!" and he dismissed the unfortunate Codadad with a curt wave of his hand.

Codadad armed himself with his glinting scimitar of gold, slung his bow and quiver of silver-tipped arrows across his back, mounted his great white horse and set off to find his forty-nine brothers.

He had travelled across desert and mountain without sight nor sound of anyone else for several days when he came across a vast plain, empty except for a sinister-looking palace of black marble set beside a deep and swiftly flowing river. As he drew nearer to the palace, Codadad saw a most beautiful girl at one of the windows. At least she would have been beautiful, but her hair was all loose and dishevelled, her clothes were torn and tears fell unchecked down her cheeks. Codadad urged his horse nearer to the window but when he came within earshot the girl cried out to him.

"Come no closer, handsome stranger, unless you too want to be captured by the frightful warrior who lives here! He will seize you like all the others and throw you into his deep dungeons. Go now, before it is too late, I implore you!"

But Codadad was not the man to ignore anyone in distress and he stood up in his saddle so he might speak to the distressed girl. "Madam, how could I possibly walk away and leave you in such peril? I am afraid of no one and certainly not a mere warrior. I shall consider it my duty to rescue you with all haste," he said (and much more besides for he was very taken with the girl in spite of her unfortunate appearance – not to mention her predicament).

The words were scarcely out of his mouth when a thin voice behind him hissed, "You think to defeat me, do you, you son of a mangy donkey?" and there stood the frightful warrior, a cloak of midnight blue swirling round his feet.

He was an awesome sight. He was twice the height of any normal man, and he looked strong enough to uproot trees with one hand. His long black hair tumbled down his back, and his fingernails looked like talons. He raised his hand and hurled a spinning metal star with lethally sharp points at Codadad. Codadad jumped swiftly to one side and the star spun uselessly into the ground. But the warrior had already flung a black-tipped spear towards Codadad who had once more to dive out of the way. The warrior laughed but again the weapon missed. Codadad whipped his scimitar out and the sun gleamed off the glittering blade as he walked calmly towards the warrior.

The girl at the window screamed and fainted clean away as Codadad kept walking. The warrior frowned and took several steps backwards for he had a terrible secret. He was not a frightful warrior at all; he was just a great big bully who had lots of fearsome weapons that he scarcely knew how to use. It did not take Codadad long to realize this and he had soon dispatched the so-called warrior and flung his body into the river.

Codadad ran into the black marble palace and looked anxiously for the girl he had seen at the window. He sped from room to room and eventually found her, her hand to her forehead, with a dazed look on her face. She could not believe that Codadad was still alive and standing in front of her very eyes, and she laughed with delight. Codadad saw that he had been right in his estimation.

Up close she was indeed very beautiful despite needing a jolly good bath and a comb to tidy her hair. Codadad led her through the palace and out into the courtyard and, as she recovered, she told Codadad her story.

"I am the daughter of a sultan, and my name is Princess Deryabar. My father dearly wanted a son and so when I was born I was a huge disappointment to him."

Codadad smiled to himself. He knew all about fathers who wanted sons!

"Please do continue," he said to Princess Deryabar, and he took her very tiny and delicate but rather grubby hand in his.

"My father looked after me well enough, but as soon as I was old enough he proposed marrying me off to a horrid old emir who already had seven wives. So I ran away, with only our trusty Grand Vizier – who did not approve of my father's plans for my marriage – for company. We were captured together by the frightful warrior, and I think the poor old Grand Vizier is in the deep dungeons," and here Princess Deryabar broke off and looked fearfully over her shoulder. "Where is the frightful warrior?" she asked and her voice trembled again.

"Sweet and delightful Princess, do not give that miserable ant another thought. I have silenced him forever," and Codadad moved closer to her. "Now we must look for your Grand Vizier in the dungeons and then you will truly be safe again."

Princess Deryabar did not think there was much the Grand Vizier could do that Codadad had not already achieved for she had decided that she would like to marry Codadad as soon as ever possible. But she was a well brought-up sultan's daughter and so said nothing of this to Codadad.

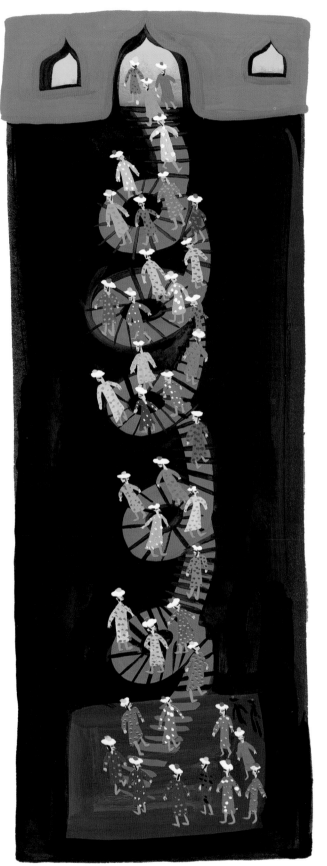

Together they walked through the black marble palace and down a steep winding staircase that led to the dungeons. Great was the rejoicing when Codadad opened the first door and found the Grand Vizier, a little thin and with an extremely untidy and straggly beard, but very happy to be reunited with Princess Deryabar. Even greater was Codadad's delight when he opened all the other doors to find that the rest of the prisoners were none other than his forty-nine brothers. They had been captured by the frightful warrior while they were hiding on their pretended hunting trip. Their pleasure at being released was much soured by the fact that it was Codadad who rescued them, and they were even more dismayed when he revealed that he was in fact their very own blood brother, the sultan's fiftieth son! But they made a good pretence of welcoming Codadad to their brotherhood, and spoke lovingly to him. The Grand Vizier perceived their false flattery, and, already very taken with Codadad's bravery and his courteous manners, resolved to discover the truth of the matter as soon as possible.

They all climbed up the steep winding staircase back into the palace. In every room they found great piles of treasure. Persian carpets, Chinese silk hangings and rare porcelain lay jumbled together anyhow, and baskets of exotic spices and perfumes were stacked in the cupboards. The brothers decided to take back as much as they could carry as gifts for their father. Great troops of camels snorted at them in the stables, and disdainfully allowed the brothers to pile up the treasure in their saddlebags. After an excellent meal, for the frightful warrior had a very well-stocked kitchen, they all set off on the long journey back to Harran.

But in the dead of night, the forty-nine brothers had a hurried conference.

"When he knows this wretched Codadad is our brother, our father the sultan will favour him even more if we tell him how we have been saved," whispered one, quite forgetting that he might have been left to rot in the frightful warrior's dungeon if Codadad had not rescued him.

"So, my brothers, we must not let any word of this rescue reach our father's ears," said another, and each of those wicked brothers crept into Codadad's tent and plunged a dagger deep into Codadad's body as he lay asleep. Before dawn they all crept away silently, scarves tied round the camel's noses to prevent them from snorting and giving the brothers away. They spared no thought for the Princess Deryabar and her aged Grand Vizier, left alone to fend for themselves in the desert.

The brothers reached Harran after a few days travelling, and the overjoyed sultan laid on a special feast to welcome them home. The treasure was unpacked and laid out for everyone to see, and the camels were given the best sweet hay and water in the palace stables. No one mentioned Codadad.

Meanwhile, back in the desert, all was not quite as the wicked brothers might have hoped for. Although gravely wounded, Codadad was not dead yet. By great good luck (or perhaps the Almighty Allah was looking after one of his favourites) a travelling doctor renowned through the land happened to pass by. The Princess Deryabar had done her best to staunch Codadad's wounds, and the Grand Vizier had frightened off the vultures who were circling the tent, by shouting all kinds of rude words at them. As a result of all their administrations, Codadad was restored enough to continue the journey to Harran.

The Princess Deryabar slipped through the city gates and managed to find a simple almshouse where she and Codadad and the Grand Vizier could stay unnoticed.

The Grand Vizier proved very adept at wheedling out gossip as he sat in the bazaar, and before long he knew the whole story of the sultan and his forty-nine sons, and he understood Codadad had indeed been telling the truth about his mother Pirouze and that he truly was the sultan's fiftieth son. With all speed he travelled to Samaria and

sought out Pirouze who was, of course, greatly relieved to have news of her dear Codadad. She travelled back with the Grand Vizier, who by now was elated but also very tired for you will remember that he was an old man and the recent exertions had taken quite a bit of the stuffing out of him. But it was all worth it when he saw the joy as Pirouze was reunited with Codadad. He was also secretly very happy to see that Pirouze was very taken with the Princess Deryabar.

Pirouze then went to the palace and demanded an audience with the sultan. She had always been one of his most favourite wives, so the sultan was delighted to see her sitting by the Peacock Fountain.

"Best of my wives, this is a most unexpected pleasure!" he exclaimed, and he ordered the servants to bring in cooling drinks and a tray of the freshest dates.

But Pirouze was not interested in such blandishments. Angrily, she told the sultan the whole terrible story and, as she did, great was the sultan's growing anger.

"Guards!" he yelled. "Fetch all my sons, all forty-nine of them, and shut the perfidious wretches up in the prison tower. Have the Palace Executioner sharpen his axe, for tomorrow they will all die!" and the frightened guards scuttled off before it was their turn to feel the sultan's wrath. He sent his finest palanquin to the humble almshouse to collect Codadad and the Princess Deryabar and her faithful Grand Vizier. With tears in his eyes he welcomed them, but for his Codadad he had no words, so great was his shame at the behaviour of his other sons. But Codadad did not want revenge and he managed to persuade the sultan to release his brothers and to cancel the executions. The sultan insisted, however, that all forty-nine of them be banished to a very far-off land for as long as they might live.

Pirouze was restored to her rightful place in the palace and named as the sultan's Number One Wife. The Grand Vizier was given a handsome apartment in the palace where he could grow orchids and gossip over coffee with the sultan's soothsayer. Codadad and the Princess Deryabar were married at the new moon, the princess in a dress of a thousand shifting colours and Codadad in a cloak of the softest brocade. Everyone in Harran was invited to the wedding and the celebrations went on until the next new moon. And everyone did indeed live happily ever after, except perhaps the forty-nine brothers who fumed and grumbled every day of their long and lonely lives.

The Wonderful Bag

he bazaar was a hubbub of activity, and everywhere rare and precious goods were laid out on the stalls. Rich, gorgeously coloured silks and velvet carpets lay tumbled in glorious profusion. Sunlight glinted off silver platters and great wine jugs, and the air was filled with exotic scents from the spice market. Peddlers wandered up and down the crowded streets, their harsh cries echoing off the rooftops like the calls of strange birds.

At a leather stall, the stallholder looked over his saddles and travelling bags and sword belts and, as he watched, a man in the flowing robes of a desert horseman picked up a bag and tucked it firmly under his arm with no attempt to hide what he was doing.

The stallholder leapt to his feet. "Son of a worthless washerwoman, replace that bag immediately!" he yelled in fury.

"Do you address me, you mangy cur? The bag is mine," said the horseman looking down his nose, and he strode off down the crowded street.

The stallholder ran after him, shouting at the top of his voice, "Summon the caliph! This rascally rat's tail has stolen one of my bags."

And soon all the stallholders were pressing round the horseman, jostling and pushing. The noise was deafening, and so it was not too long before the guards appeared. The stallholder and the horseman were both hauled off, loudly protesting all the way and calling each other all manner of rude names:

"Festering flea of a mule!"

"Impudent and scrawny she-cat!" and so on.

The caliph looked at the bag and then at the horseman and then at the stallholder. "A simple matter. All that is required is that you should both tell me what is in the bag, and I shall then open it. Whoever has told the truth shall retain the bag. The other I will leave to consider his ways in the dungeon," and the caliph looked at both men expectantly.

"Well, that is an easy matter to resolve," said the horseman quickly. "In the bag you will find a glass of foaming sherbet, a chess set, a rare flying carpet, a silver flute, a guinea fowl and a very smelly goat's cheese."

Well! The stallholder was utterly astonished by this curious list of items. He knew perfectly well that the bag was empty, but he had no wish to be outdone, so he replied, "Almighty Caliph, it is quite clear this son of an ancient camel-driver is lying. In the bag you will find ten yellow silk turbans, a bottle of wine from Egypt, several pomegranates and a dozen oysters, a scimitar of exceptional sharpness, a golden eagle and a saddle of polished red leather."

The horseman snorted in disgust. "O, wise Caliph, this baboon did not give me time to finish. As well as the items I have already mentioned, you will find a basket of freshly-picked dates, a blue pond of exceptional clarity, several dancing girls, an orange grove, a thousand lit candles, an emerald as big as an ostrich egg, a sea captain and a she-bear."

The stallholder bowed even lower to the caliph and declared, "By the beard of my ancient father, did I mention the whirling dervish, the orchid flower pavilion, the blue mosque of Istanbul, the spouting whale, a company of fierce Turkish soldiers, the alchemist's stone, a troubadour and a grove of lime trees?"

"Stop, stop!" shrieked the caliph. "Either this bag is quite bottomless or you two are attempting to make a fool of me and of the law."

The caliph opened the bag and held it upside down. Onto the floor fell two sugared almonds, and absolutely nothing else. The caliph's eyebrows came together in a deep frown and as he drew in his breath to speak, the stallholder said very quickly, "A thousand, thousand pardons, greatly revered Caliph. I see I have been quite mistaken. This is clearly not my bag. I must depart with all due haste to find my own bag with its most valuable contents." And so saying he swept out of the court, leaving the thieving horseman to his fate.

Sinbad and the Island of Elephants

 inbad had travelled the high seas all his life and had fantastical and hair-raising exploits to recount in the coffee shops of the bazaar. But as he had grown older, he had resolved to lead a quiet life as far away from ships as possible. The caliph, however, had other ideas. One day, as Sinbad was snoozing gently on his divan by the deep blue pool in his outer courtyard, there came a thunderous knocking at the door, and soon a very superior-looking courtier loftily informed Sinbad that the caliph desired to see him. With a sinking heart, Sinbad pushed his feet into his tasselled slippers and combed his beard. He felt sure his quiet life was about to be disrupted.

Sure enough, the caliph wanted Sinbad to take special gifts and felicitations to the King of Serendib. Serendib was far across the seas and the voyage there would be long and hazardous.

"But, Most Noble and Wondrous Commander of the Faithful, I have resolved never to leave Baghdad again," Sinbad explained to the caliph. "My voyages in the service of your Most Illustrious Personage have taken me all over the world, through many a tempest and earthquake. I have fought strange and supernatural forces, I have duelled with giant man-eating birds and tricked huge giants. I have brought you great riches in precious stones and gold, fine silks from the Orient and spices from the darkest jungles. I am an old man, all I want now is my supper on time and my own bed to sleep in, believe me, Esteemed Caliph," and he bowed so low his turban brushed the carpet.

The caliph drew his eyebrows together in a ferocious scowl. "Am I to understand that you are refusing to perform this small service for me?" he growled from the depths of his magnificent beard.

And, of course, Sinbad found himself saying, "Most Noble of Masters, this most insignificant of sailors would not dare to refuse your slightest wish. I will sail on the next tide," and bowing very deeply again, he retreated out of the caliph's presence. All the way home he muttered in his heart at his weakness but he soon found himself on board his great sailing ship, skimming the waves on the way to Serendib. All went well, and after an uneventful voyage, Sinbad presented himself at the court of the King of Serendib and unpacked the gifts from the caliph.

The gifts were indeed splendid. There was a complete suit of armour of beaten gold; fifty silk robes so fine that the material felt like butterfly wings; one hundred bales of pure hand-woven white linen; a drinking vessel of the finest agate; and a tablet of stone which, it was said, had belonged to the great Solomon himself. And there were countless other ordinary things like a carved jade peacock and a kite of exceptional swiftness and a pair of silver slippers with gold heels, so tiny that only the most delicate of princesses could have worn them. The King of Serendib was delighted, and not a little overwhelmed. So much so that Sinbad found it very difficult to take his leave, but eventually the king relented and, having showered Sinbad with many costly presents, waved him farewell.

Unfortunately for Sinbad his departure did not go unnoticed, and he was only three days at sea when his ship was set upon by pirates who had heard of the considerable booty on board. The pirates helped themselves to all the riches from the king, commandeered the ship and cast Sinbad and his sailors ashore on a remote island.

They were most fortunately rescued by a rich merchant who lived in a very grand house with many rooms and pavilions. Now this merchant bought and sold ivory, and he made it clear that in exchange for rescuing him, he expected Sinbad to help him in this wicked trade. He took Sinbad to a great tree deep in the forest and told him to climb to the highest branch. Then when the elephants came by, he was to shoot them and then remove their tusks. This Sinbad did for several days, and he soon had a large pile of ivory for the merchant.

But then one night, a very strange thing happened. Instead of walking by the tall tree where Sinbad was hiding, the elephants all gathered round the foot of the tree and began shaking it with their huge bodies. So great was the motion set up by the elephants that Sinbad fell out of the tree. As he plummeted towards the earth, he was sure his last hour had come, so you can imagine his surprise when he felt himself caught very carefully by several trunks. One elephant then placed him high up on her back and with a soothing swaying motion began walking through the forest.

Curiously Sinbad realized that he did not feel afraid; somehow he trusted the great gentle beasts.

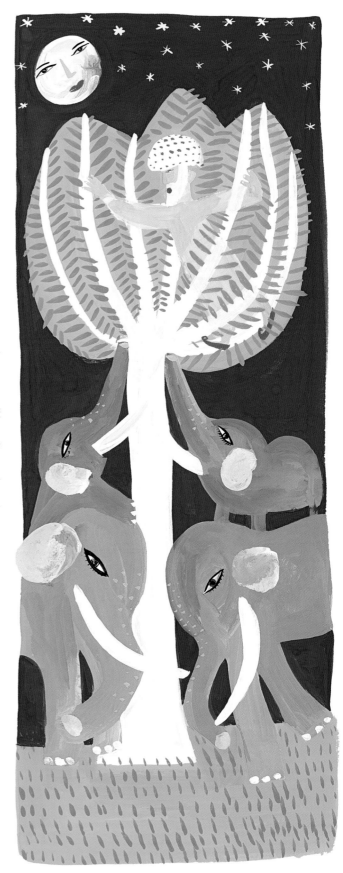

After a long time they came to a clearing and the elephant lifted Sinbad down to the ground. All around lay the huge skulls and bones of elephants – it was an elephant graveyard. The elephants nudged Sinbad towards the bones and suddenly he realized what they were trying to tell him.

"By the beard of the prophet!" cried Sinbad. "I see what these wise beasts are telling me. Why kill living creatures when here is enough to keep the merchant in great wealth for years to come?" And so Sinbad smiled at the elephants and bowed so low that his turban brushed the grass at his feet. The elephants trumpeted their joy round the forest and then carried Sinbad back to the great tree where he found the merchant waiting for him most anxiously.

"Sinbad, noble mariner!" he cried. "When I heard that great trumpeting call, I thought to find you dead, crushed beneath the feet of these monstrous creatures. But here you are, unhurt and most miraculously riding on the back of one."

"May you and all your sons live in great prosperity for ever more," murmured Sinbad politely. "These noble creatures have never wished me any ill. Indeed they have shared a great secret with me which will bring you untold wealth," and Sinbad explained to the merchant that he need never kill another elephant as long as he lived.

Of course the merchant wanted to shower Sinbad with money and ivory beyond imagining but, as we know, Sinbad had only one desire in his heart – to have his supper on time and to sleep in his own bed. So the merchant promised Sinbad a place on the next ship that called to collect the ivory. And before the moon had waxed and waned twice, Sinbad stood once more in Baghdad, in front of the caliph. He bowed very deeply and offered the caliph all manner of salutations and gracious greetings. He also presented him with a vast quantity of ivory which made the caliph very happy indeed.

"I can see that this was a most profitable voyage, faithful Sinbad. Perhaps now you have most truly earned your quiet years of repose," and the caliph then summoned the Keeper of the Treasury Purse and gave Sinbad a very large bag of gold indeed, and several silver sherbet glasses and a singing bird of the utmost sweetness and a carpet of the finest wool and several pomegranate trees and a finely carved screen and other such trifles. Sinbad staggered away home bearing all these gifts, and, after an extremely good night's sleep in his own bed, he was to be found in the bazaar, telling everyone of his adventures on the Island of Elephants, a cup of the very best coffee by his side.

The Enchanted Horse

any moons ago there lived in Persia an emperor who was fascinated by science and geometry and all things mechanical. Above all he loved anything that was fabulous and rare, and so it was that his palace courtyard was always filled with strange inventors and magicians, all seeking to attract the emperor's attention. Many were the gifts presented to the emperor — mechanical birds that sang without stopping, orchids that bloomed a different colour every morning, sand clocks and marble fountains that ran with rainbow coloured water, sherbet glasses made of diamonds, illuminated books that spoke when opened. The treasure house was full to the roof, and the court vizier was tearing his hair out trying to display each curiosity where the emperor could see it whenever he wished.

It was the emperor's birthday. After his breakfast he was carried out to the courtyard on his peacock throne. He looked magnificent. His robes were of the finest spun gold silk, and his crown, which was studded with emeralds, glittered in the sunlight. There was a rush as people surged forward to present their gifts. The air was filled with music and bells, and birdsong mingled with shouts and pleas as everyone tried to catch the emperor's attention. Sweet perfumes wafted everywhere and the pavements were strewn with flower petals. There was an air of huge excitement.

Then the crowds parted and a sudden silence fell. A very strange and ugly old man approached, leading a great black horse. As they drew near, the emperor could see that the horse was not real but made of highly polished ebony. The old man, who was in fact a powerful and evil magician, knelt down and kissed the ground before the peacock throne.

"What is this noble beast that you bring before me today?" asked the emperor. "I presume it has some hidden secret."

"Indeed, O, Most Magnificent Emperor," murmured the old man, "this is a flying horse. It will carry any rider wherever he wishes to go in the entire world."

Now for all his delight in wondrous things, the emperor would never believe any claim until he had seen it with his own eyes. "This is truly an extraordinary beast if what you claim is true," he said to the old man. "Mount your horse and bring me a bamboo shoot from the grove that lies at the bottom of the mountains over there," said the emperor, pointing into the far distance. The old man bowed deeply, mounted the horse which rose into the air within seconds and flew over the heads of the astonished crowd. Moments later, they were back, and the old man laid a fresh bamboo shoot at the foot of the peacock throne. The emperor was delighted. "Your horse is indeed a rare beast. What reward can I offer in return for this gift?" he said excitedly.

"I wish for only two things," said the old man with a sly smile that the emperor did not quite like. "Ten caskets of gold and the hand of your daughter, Princess Jasmeen, in marriage."

Everyone was aghast. Not least the emperor, who wanted the ebony horse very much indeed, but was certainly not prepared to give away his lovely daughter to a stranger. "You shall have your gold.

You may even have twenty caskets, but do not ask for my daughter. That is impossible."
Princess Jasmeen began to weep as the old man argued with the emperor. She could see
how much her father wanted the ebony horse but she did not like the look of the old
man one little bit.

Now Princess Jasmeen's brother, Prince Yusuf, had been watching the old man very
carefully and had noticed that when the old man had mounted the ebony horse he turned
a peg high up on the left-hand side of the horse's neck. Thinking that his father might
have a better chance of convincing the old man to accept the twenty caskets of gold if the
horse was not by his side, the prince leapt onto its back and turned the peg. The horse
soared high up into the skies and vanished from sight.

Everyone started to talk at once. The emperor shouted for his guards to arrest the old
man, but he had slipped away in all the hubbub. Princess Jasmeen was delighted that she
had been spared an awful marriage, but she was distraught at the disappearance of her
brother. The empress had fainted and her servant girls were wailing in distress.

The vizier shook his head gravely and went back to dusting the mechanical birds. It was a sorry ending to the emperor's birthday.

Meanwhile, what of Prince Yusuf? He and the ebony horse flew through the air and he marvelled as he saw all of Persia laid out like a carpet far below. But after a while he realized with a cold shiver that he had absolutely no idea whatsoever how to bring the horse down to the ground again. He twisted the peg this way and that, but it made no difference. In a panic he felt all around the horse's neck and finally, to his joy, he discovered another peg on the right-hand side. He turned this and slowly, slowly, the horse began to float downwards.

He spotted a huge glittering palace laid out in a beautiful garden, full of fountains and statues. "I am sure once I explain who I am that all will be well and I can return to my father who must be very anxious about my safety," he thought. And so he brought the ebony horse down gently, landing behind a gilded pavilion beside a blue pool. He could hear gentle laughter and soft voices and so he peeped round the edge of the golden screens.

Rich silk cushions were piled around the pool and there sat the most beautiful girl Yusuf had ever seen. She was obviously a king's daughter. Her servants sat nearby, chatting as they sipped sherbet and nibbled sweetmeats.

Prince Yusuf stepped round the screen. The girls screamed, but the princess looked calmly at the handsome stranger who appeared to have dropped from the sky. "Young man, do you normally arrive unannounced and unattended?" She could see from his clothes that he was someone of consequence, but where were his servants?

Prince Yusuf bowed deeply. "Most beautiful flower of the desert, you see before you Prince Yusuf, son of the Emperor of Persia. I have come here on an enchanted horse and I descended to your palace wishing only to refresh myself. But you have quite stolen my heart, and I find I cannot leave without at least knowing your name, O, pearl of the deepest ocean." (He had quite a way with words, young Prince Yusuf.)

"I am Princess Laila, and my father has promised me in marriage to the Prince of India. I doubt he will be very pleased to discover you here," but the princess smiled very deeply into Yusuf's eyes as she said this. "The Prince of India is very old," she added.

"Then come with me! My enchanted horse will transport us back to Persia, and my father will welcome you as my bride," cried Yusuf, conveniently forgetting that his father might have other things on his mind.

Princess Laila rose gracefully from her cushions and accepted Prince Yusuf's hand as he led her to the ebony horse. He placed her gently on the horse's back, climbed up behind her and twisted the left-hand peg on the horse's neck. They rose into the sky and swiftly turned towards Persia. The horse sped through the night as the stars glittered around them, and the moonlight gleamed on the ebony horse. As dawn was breaking, Prince Yusuf twisted the right-hand peg and they began to descend. Now he had decided that he could not arrive with his beautiful princess unannounced, and so he brought the horse down in the Summer Palace outside the city.

There he left Laila to rest while he went ahead to prepare for her arrival. Unfortunately they had been seen by the evil magician, who had never ceased scanning the skies by day and night, looking for his lost ebony horse.

The magician put on his very best robes and approached the princess. Bowing deeply, he told her the prince had sent him to bring her into the city. "The most noble prince felt you might not know how to control the horse. I am the only other person who understands how it works," smiled the magician. This was true, of course, but the poor princess did not know why. She mounted the horse behind the magician and up, up into the air they flew.

Far below, Princess Laila could see a huge palace of sparkling white marble. She also saw a great procession of horses and camels pouring out of the palace gates, guarded by smart soldiers with polished scimitars glinting, and at the head of the procession was her own Prince Yusuf! Then Laila knew that she had been tricked by the wicked old man. She started to cry.

"None of that nonsense!" the magician growled. "I built this magic horse but your precious prince stole it from me, and so I have stolen his bride," and he turned the horse far, far away from the palace.

It seemed to the unhappy princess that they flew for ever. Dusk was falling when the magician finally landed the horse on the edge of a dark forest. They had reached the kingdom of Greece. As it happened, the king was riding home after a day's hunting. He and his guards spotted the magician and Princess Laila just as the magician had conjured up a fire to cook supper. The king did not like the look of the magician (you will remember he was very ugly) but he was quite enchanted with the princess, so, when she flung herself at his feet and poured out some terrible story of enchanted horses and being kidnapped, he was quite prepared to believe her. The king had the magician thrown into the very deepest dungeon and that is the last we shall hear of him in this story. But the princess he took back to his palace and settled her in his finest guest apartment.

The ebony horse he put into the treasure house, just to keep it out of the way, not realizing that it was indeed a very great treasure.

The next morning the princess arose refreshed and with a glad heart. She felt sure the King of the Greeks would help her return to Persia and all her troubles would be over. But, alas, the King of the Greeks decided that *he* should marry Laila and had arranged the ceremony for later that afternoon. "I am sure when you think about it you will see that this is a very agreeable arrangement," he encouraged the princess as she was taken, weeping copiously, back to the finest guest apartment.

Once safely alone, the princess stopped crying and began to think just how she might get out of this awful predicament. She decided to pretend she was mad, and so it was that when the servant girls came to dress her for the wedding, they found her shrieking and yelling, tearing her hair and scratching anyone who came near her. The wedding was postponed for a few days.

In the meantime a distracted Prince Yusuf was wandering around Persia looking for his lost bride. She seemed to have vanished off the face of the earth. And then one day he overheard a conversation between some merchants in a bazaar.

"Has the King of the Greeks married his beautiful princess yet?" asked one.

"No, I hear she is still as mad as the mists," said another.

"And is it true that she arrived in Greece on an ebony horse?" asked a third.

Prince Yusuf begged the merchants to tell him all about the King of the Greeks and his mad bride, and most importantly, the name of the city where his beloved Princess Laila was to be found.

The prince saddled up his horse and galloped without stopping through day and through night until he reached the city. There he disguised himself as a doctor and presented himself at the court of the King of the Greeks.

"Your visit is very timely, Doctor," said the king. "I am to be married to the most beautiful damsel but she is in a state of deep distress and no one will go near her for fear of injury. Great will be your reward if you can cure her."

The king took Yusuf to the guest apartment. Even from a distance, Yusuf could hear the sound of breaking pottery and a great wailing. A dishevelled servant came out, locking the door very carefully behind him.

"How is my poor desert lily today?" asked the king anxiously.

"She grows worse, O, Most Magnificent King," replied the servant, and Yusuf noticed a long scratch on the king's arm.

"You see," said the king. "I despair she will ever recover. Please do what you can."

Yusuf unlocked the door and slipped inside. A scene of utter devastation met his eyes. Shards of broken pottery littered the carpet and feathers blew everywhere from torn cushions. Curtains hung in tatters around the windows, and tables and chairs were upturned on the floor. The princess had clearly made a very good job of pretending to be mad. She was crouched in a corner; her hair looked like a bird's nest and her dress was torn. As Yusuf drew near she began wailing again, but when she recognized who it was, she stopped mid-shriek.

"Is that truly you, O, light of my heart?" she asked, hardly daring to believe that it was truly her Prince Yusuf.

"O, delight of my eyes, it is! How clever you have been! But you must pretend a little while longer so I can arrange our escape," murmured Yusuf. "I will arrange for the ebony horse to be ready and we will make good our escape. Have courage, my best beloved," and he rumpled his clothes and knocked his turban askew before slipping out of the door, and returning to the king who was standing anxiously waiting.

"Most Noble King, I perceive exactly what is wrong with your bride. She is possessed by a djinn and it is my view that this djinn can only be removed by means of the enchanted horse upon which she arrived. Please arrange for the horse and the princess to be taken to the lakeside. I will need several great fires lit so that the smoke may drive out the djinn," and Yusuf bowed very low to hide his smile.

The king was delighted and made the necessary arrangements with all speed. The ebony horse was brought to the lakeside. Huge fires were lit and as the smoke rose high the princess was brought out by the king's guards. Yusuf walked round the fires, muttering incantations, went up to the horse and shouted a few words in Persian.

"You see what a great doctor this is," whispered the king to the chief of the guards. "He has many tongues at his command."

Yusuf took the princess in his arms and placed her on the horse. He jumped behind her and, almost hidden by the smoke, he reached up to the horse's neck and turned the left-hand peg. The horse rose high in the night sky, and, before the astounded king and his guards really understood what was happening, Prince Yusuf and Princess Laila were far out of sight.

The prince guided the horse towards Persia, and this time landed safely within the walls of his father's palace. The emperor was overjoyed to see his son once more, and the empress fainted again but this time it was from sheer delight. Prince Yusuf and Princess Laila were married the very next morning and the feasting went on for several days.

The prince had sent messengers to Laila's father, bearing many gifts and an invitation to join in the celebrations, so everyone was happy. The enchanted horse was placed in the main courtyard for all to see, but no one was even slightly tempted to ride it again. And so they all lived for ever afterwards in great contentment.

How Queen Sheherezade and King Shahriyar Lived Happily Ever After

For one thousand nights Sheherezade entertained Shahriyar with her wonderful stories. She told him the story of *The Birds and the Beasts and the Carpenter* and *What a Drop of Honey Caused*. She told him about *The Serpent Queen* and *The Tomcat and the Mouse*. The king listened spellbound as she related *The History of the Young King of the Black Isles* and the story of *Sidi Nouman* and the tale of *Princess Budur, Moon of Moons*. And not forgetting the tale of *Zumurrud the Beautiful and Ali Shar, Son of Glory*. O, the list was endless! And Sheherezade was always careful to break off her tale just as the sun rose, at the most exciting part, so her life was spared for another night.

But on the thousand and first night she finished the tale of *The Enchanted Horse* just as dawn was breaking. She sat with her hands folded in her lap and looked at the king with a gentle smile.

"For one thousand nights, O, Noble King, I have regaled you with my tales. I have made you laugh, I have made you gasp with wonder and I have made you cry with sadness at the foolishness of men. I have sent you travelling on magic carpets to fabled lands. I have wafted the air with exotic smells of spices and blossom as my stories took you through busy bazaars and peaceful gardens. I have filled your sleep with myriad dreams of djinns and magic lamps and great horses flying through the sky. And as the stars have faded from the lightening sky over the minarets of this palace you have given me another day to live. Now I have no stories left to tell."

And as she fell silent, Shahriyar realized that never once had Sheherezade failed him or asked for reward or thought of herself. And he was ashamed.

"Most excellent of women, I have long forgotten my evil vow undertaken in great anger, so powerful has been the spell of your storytelling. How may I beg your forgiveness?" he asked.

"Please, O, Great King, all I ask is that you give me your assurance that no ill will befall my beloved father," whispered Sheherezade.

"I shall do more than assure you of that. Your noble father will remain by my side as my Grand Vizier for the rest of his life!" cried the king. "And then we shall have a proper wedding feast, and you and I shall live in peace together forever."

And so it happened.

You might think that was the end of the story, but King Shahriyar had one more request of his queen.

"Now, most clever and ingenious weaver of magic, please start again at the very beginning for I wish to hear all the tales once more," he commanded, his eyes alight with mischief.

And so Sheherezade began, "Once upon a far off time, there lived two brothers in an old city in Persia..."

About the author and illustrator

FIONA WATERS is an established anthologist and author of over fifty books, particularly well known for her poetry collections and gifted retellings of classic tales including *The Selfish Giant*, *Mythical Beasts* and the Pavilion title *Wizard Tales*. She has also worked in the children's publishing world for many years – testimony to her broad knowledge of children's books and poetry – as a publisher and a bookseller, as a consultant for television and radio, and as a judge of several book prizes. Fiona lives in a seventeenth-century cottage in Dorset with thousands of books and almost as many cats!

CHRISTOPHER CORR was born in London and trained in Graphic Design at Manchester Polytechnic before completing an MA in Illustration at the Royal College of Art. Christopher has travelled extensively in Europe, Asia and Africa. He has won several awards, including the Royal College of Art Drawing Prize, and has had many international one-man shows, including his Looking East Looking West exhibition at the Berkeley Square Gallery. As well as illustrating children's books, he has worked on many different commissions, including magazine and newspaper features, a Royal Mail postage stamp and numerous posters, paintings and prints.